What Friends Do

by Miriam Sklar

ISBN: 978-1-338-75086-7
Illustrated by John Lund

Published by Scholastic Inc., 557 Broadway, New York, NY 10012

10 9 8 7 6 5 4 68 25 26 27/0

Printed in Jiaxing, China. First printing, January 2021.

Friends ride.

Friends slide.

Friends sing.

Friends swing.

Friends bake.

Friends skate.

Friends read!